For Stanley Becker

Library of Congress Cataloging-in-Publication Data

Coplans, Peta.
Dottie / written and illustrated by Peta Coplans. – 1st American ed. p. cm.
Summary: Dottie the dog persists in her love of gardening, even though her parents think it is improper behavior for a canine.
ISBN 0-395-66788-7
[1. Dogs–Fiction. 2. Gardening–Fiction. 3. Behavior–Fiction.]
I. Title.
PZ7.C7914Do   1994
[E] – dc20

92-41955
CIP
AC

Copyright © 1993 by Peta Coplans
First American edition 1994
Originally published in Great Britain in 1993 by
Andersen Press Ltd.

Printed in Italy

10 9 8 7 6 5 4 3 2 1

Dottie

Written and illustrated by
Peta Coplans

Houghton Mifflin Company Boston 1994

Dottie was always growing things. It drove her parents crazy.
She started in the garden.
"Not in the GARDEN!" said Dad.
"Gardens are for burying bones and rolling in the grass."

She grew things in the house.
"Not in the HOUSE, Dottie!" said Mom
"Look at this muddy carpet!"

"Dogs don't grow things," said Mom and Dad together.
"Who says?" asked Dottie.
"EVERYONE!" said Mom and Dad.
"Now be a good dog. Go out and chase a postman, instead."

Dottie went to visit Duck.
He was putting on his rollerskates.
"Ducks don't rollerskate!" said Dottie.

"Don't they?" said Duck.

"I do."

On the way to Rabbit's house, Dottie saw Cat.

"What are you doing?" said Dottie. "Cats don't like water."

"Don't they?" said Cat.

"I do."

Rabbit was mixing colors when Dottie arrived.

"You can't do that!" said Dottie. "Rabbits don't paint pictures."

"Don't they?" said Rabbit. "I do."

Dottie went home. She knew what she was going to do.

A few nights later, Dad sat up in bed. He woke Mom.
"Listen!" he said, "I hear strange noises outside."

"It could be a burglar!" said Mom.
They sneaked downstairs.

In the furthest corner of the garden, they found the answer.
"It's me," said Dottie. "I'm growing things."
"Go to bed IMMEDIATELY!" said Dad.
"This MINUTE!" said Mom
"And no more growing things," they said together.
"Dogs don't grow things!"
Dottie went to bed, but Mom and Dad couldn't sleep.

"Why can't she be like other dogs?" Dad sighed.
"She IS very good at growing things," said Mom.
"Couldn't she have a few little plants? I saw strawberries."
"I LOVE fresh strawberries!" said Dad.
"And lettuce," said Mom, "And lovely runner beans!"
"Go to sleep!" said Dad. "You're making me hungry!"

It was Dottie's birthday a few weeks later.
Rabbit, Cat and Duck were all invited to her party.
After cake and lemonade, Dottie took her friends outside.

"Look!" she said. "It's from Mom and Dad."
"That's a big present," said Cat. "What is it?"
"Open it!" shouted Rabbit. "Let's see what's inside!"
"I think it's a giant bone! All dogs love those," said Duck.

"A watering can!" said Cat. "You don't need THAT!"
"Or flower pots, or seeds, OR a rake!" said Duck.
"EVERYONE knows dogs don't grow things," said Rabbit.

"Don't they?" said Mom.
"Don't they?" said Dad.

"Don't they?" said Dottie.

THE
END